Bunnies!!!

Kevan Atteberry

KT KATHERINE TEGEN BOOKS
An Imprint of HarperCollins Publishers

Hello, tree.

For my most amazing agent, Erin. Thank you!
I am so happy (and lucky) we crossed paths.
For my terrific sons, Lennon and Rio. I love you guys.
For my lovely wife, Teri. I hope you recognize this
when I finally put it in your hands.

Katherine Tegen Books is an imprint of HarperCollins Publishers.

Bunnies!!!
Copyright © 2015 by Kevan Atteberry. All rights reserved. Printed in the United States of America.
No part of this book may be used or reproduced in any manner whatsoever without
written permission except in the case of brief quotations embodied in critical
articles and reviews. For information address HarperCollins Children's Books,
a division of HarperCollins Publishers, 195 Broadway, New York, NY 10007.
www.harpercollinschildrens.com

ISBN 978-0-06-230783-5 (trade bdg.)

The artist used Adobe Photoshop to create the digital illustrations for this book.
Typography by Erica De Chavez.
15 16 17 18   PC   10 9 8 7 6 5 4 3 2
❖
First Edition

Hello, butterfly.

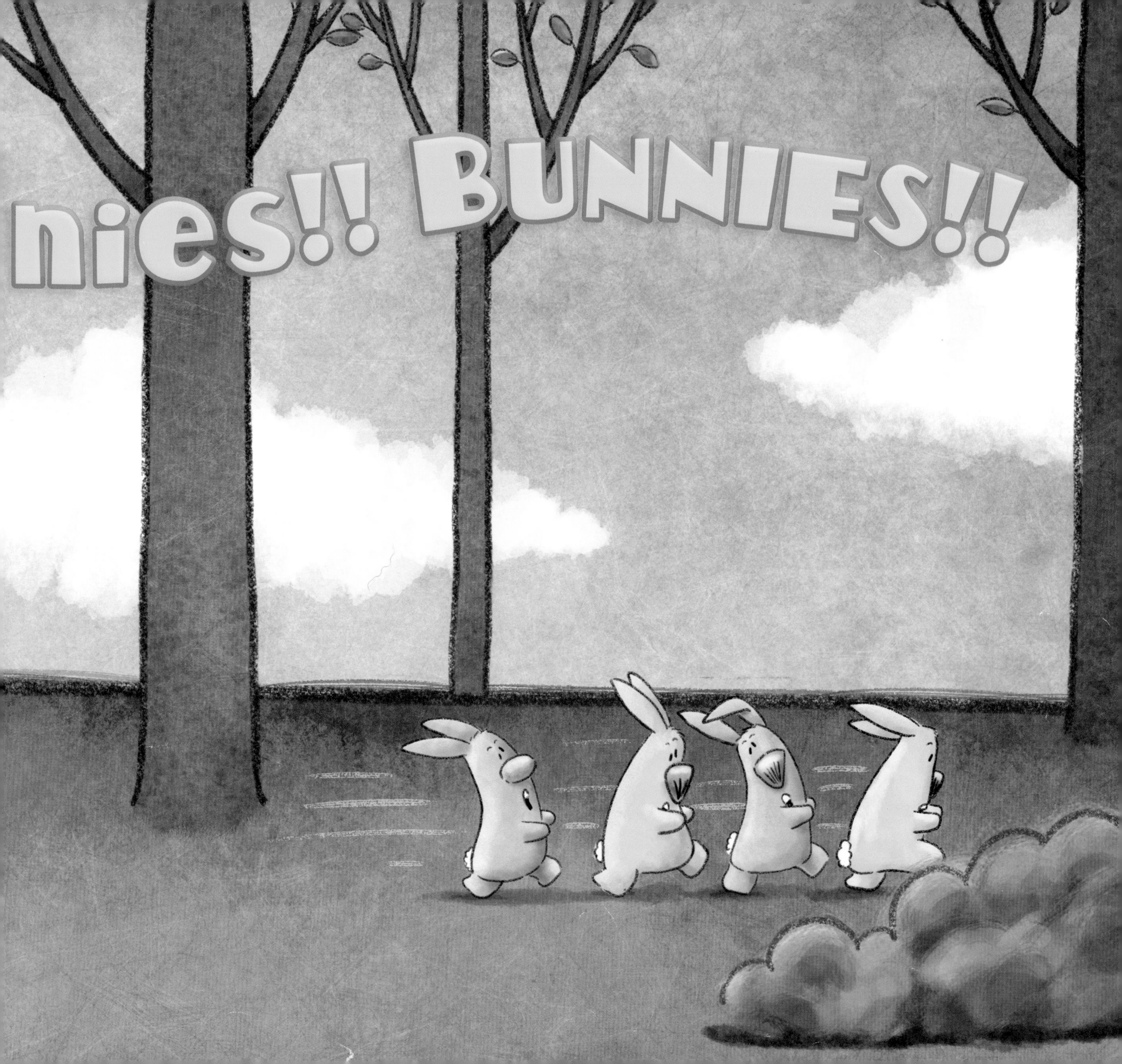
nies!! BUNNIES!!

Hello, stump.

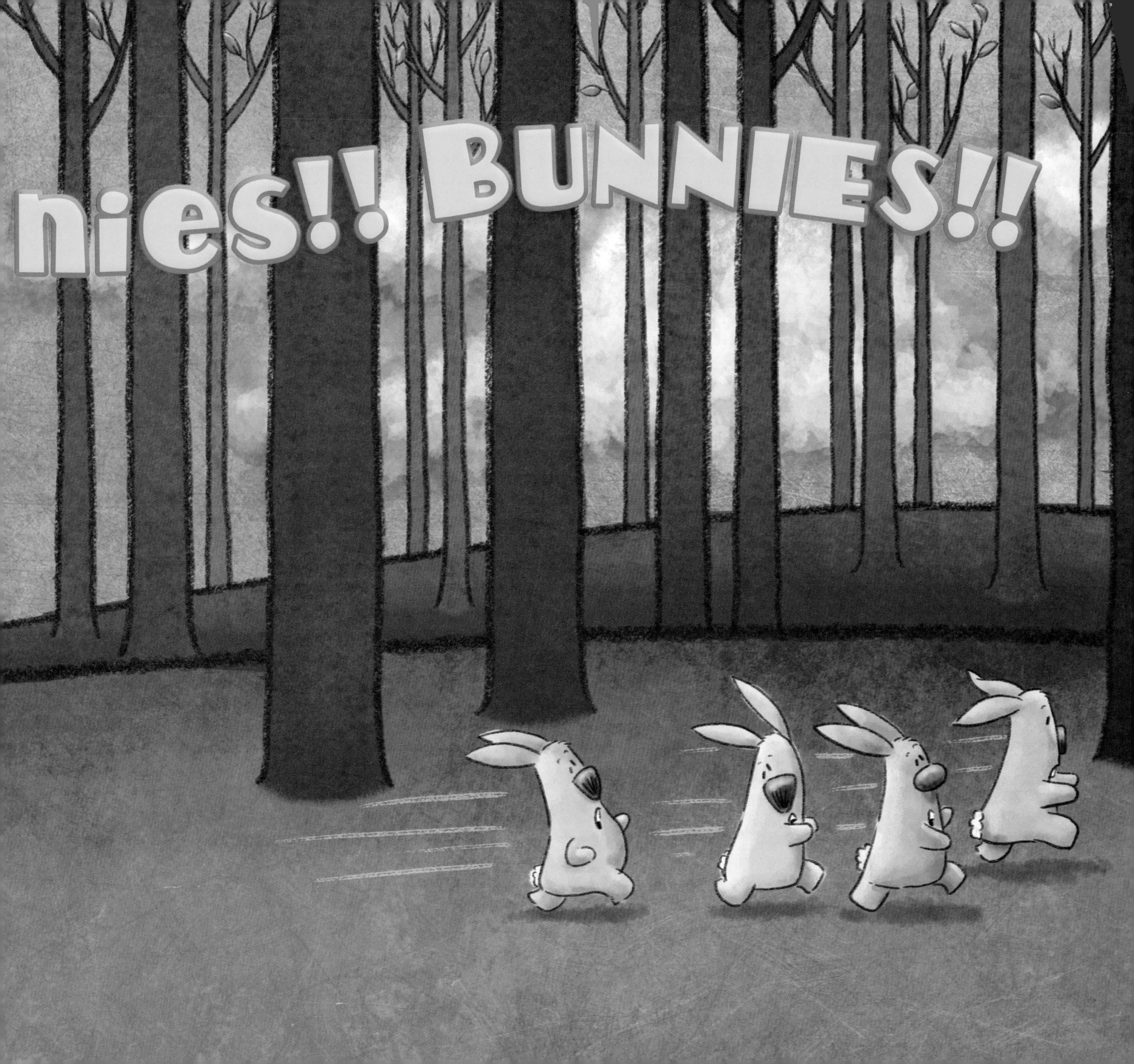
nies!! BUNNIES!!

Bunnies?

Bunnies?

Bunnies?

Nooooo bunnies.

Bunnies!

Bunnies!